Clutching a Beating Heart

J. Adams

Cover Design by Laura J. Miller

www.anauthorsart.com

I've heard it said that the Carolina Mountains date back to the time of Christ–that they were His mountains. I've often wondered if The Master ever comes back to His mountains, and if He does, what He must think of the things going on within the green, majestic rolling peaks. I'm guessing He's probably visited a time or two and is likely saddened by the deeds the mountains have witnessed. The whispers of what they know echo all around us. Does anyone ever listen? Or even care? We should, for the Smokey hills see clearly what others assume is hidden.

And the mountains never lie.

It's a Long, Long Road

As the sun beats down on the dry grass, a sparse amount of clothing lay littering the front lawn. An old tote bag is tossed from behind the screen door.

"Get your slutty behind off my property, and don't ever come back!"

"But Dina, I didn't do nothin'. It ain't my fault."

"The hell if you didn't. I know what happened, so don't try to lie to me. I ain't dumb, I got eyes!"

"Please, Dina. I ain't got nowhere to go."

"That ain't my problem. You shoulda thought of that before, you skank!"

"But Dina, please listen– "

"I ain't interested in anything else you got to say. Now get off my property, Sonora!"

"But it's my house, too."

"Not anymore!"

"But Dina, you don't know–"

"I said I don't wanna hear it! Go on, get off!"

"I ain't goin'. It's my house, too."

"Girl, if you step back up in here, you got a world of hurtin' coming. You don't believe me, you just try it. Now get your slutbag behind on outta here!"

The slamming door echoes off houses as more neighbors perch on porches, taking everything in. Nothing that happens in the small southern town is ever private. Several pairs of eyes watch the lone figure tearfully gather her few belongings before slowly making her way down the road leading from town. Some shake their heads in pity, while others congregate and murmur, "She had it coming."

But one old soul stands in her doorway with tears streaming down her cheeks as she watches the young woman reach the street corner, and then turn, disappearing from sight. Glancing over at her husband where he stands by the window gazing down the road, she watches his jaw clench and prays for him, as well as the girl. It is all she can do.

* * *

You know that old saying 'Keep your friends close and your enemies closer?' Well Mama used to say, "Keep your friends close and your enemies as far away as possible." As I walk up this long stretch of highway in the scorching summer heat, making my way to Asheville–forty miles away–I'm finally grasping the wisdom of Mama's words. The closer you keep an enemy, the quicker that trust can bite you in the behind. My youngest sister Kelly latched on to Mama's words quickly. She left two years ago, just three months after Mama passed. I haven't heard from her since. Not even a phone call or letter.

Securing the tote bag on one shoulder, I slip my purse from the other, grateful I was able to grab it before being shoved out of the house. My sister has always had the temper of a wild boar, but this is the first time I have ever experienced her full wrath.

Checking the contents of my purse, I release a deep sigh. I have no money on me, but I do have the small box of jewelry Mama gave me before she passed, and the gold bracelet Mama's friend, Mrs. Tilly, gave me before she died last month. I also have a few hundred in the bank in savings, so I'm not broke.

I miss old Mrs. Tilly. Up until she died, she was my best friend in Old Fort. She always watched out for me and I spent more time at her place than my own. I came to depend on her. She was the only person I *could* depend on.

Because she knew my secrets.

"I wish you were here now, Mrs. Tilly, because I don't know where I'm goin' or what I'm doin'."

I'm here, precious baby.

Smiling, I resist the urge to close my eyes as I absorb her comforting soft voice. This is the third time I've felt her near this past few weeks. I sense Mama near every now and then, but never as often as her oldest and dearest friend.

"Where do I go, Mrs. Tilly?"

For a moment there is nothing, and I scold myself for being silly enough to think she will answer the question. Then I hear her voice, the tone as firm as if we are talking across her kitchen table from one another.

Townsend, precious. Cutter Gap in Townsend.

* * *

After three miles and no luck catching a ride, I am exhausted, my strength almost spent.

I don't know if I'm gonna make it, Mrs. Tilly. I stop a minute to catch my breath and wait for a stomach cramp to ease.

You'll make it, baby. Hold on a little longer.

A moment later an 18-wheeler stops and a window is rolled down.

"Where you headed?" The man's voice is gruff, but his face is kind.

"To Asheville."

"I'm stopping there to drop off a shipment. Hop in."

Thank you, Lord.

J. Adams

To Carve a Life

Townsend, Tennessee

One month later.

Birds perched in the surrounding trees serenade me as I sweep the front porch. These same trees offer me privacy from the prying eyes of nearby neighbors- privacy that I continually crave.

Driving up the long country road last month, the little cabin on Cutter Gap had stood out like a beacon and I immediately called the number on the 'For Rent' sign. Fifteen minutes later, the owner came, showed me the inside of the furnished two bedroom home and I signed the papers. For the next six months the place is mine.

The inside is rustic-country, decorated in greens and reds. The floors and walls are wood and wooden beams run across the ceilings. Patchwork quilts cover the twin bed in one room and the king in the master suite. Twice a week, I soak my cares away in the garden tub. The screened-in back porch blesses me with a view of the woods where I frequently–well, daily, really–spot deer walking amidst the trees. Off to the side is the lake, the mist settling over it making it look magical and enchanted.

When I made it to Asheville, I got more for Mama's jewelry than I'd expected. Spotting an old Mustang for sale in the pawn shop parking lot (it belonged to the sister of the shop owner) I called the number on the front window and paid cash for it. Other than needing a new fuel filter and alternator, the car was in great condition. Having taken an automotive shop class in high school, I was able to make the repairs myself. After two days of repairs and rest, I headed to Townsend. I rented the cabin and stopped by IGA and bought some groceries. That evening I picked up a used sewing machine listed for sale in the local paper, then bought some material. Mrs. Tilly taught me how to make quilted purses and I've always supported myself with that skill. Here in Townsend, I've been selling newly-crafted purses at *Cabin Crafts*, putting the small earnings away with the rest of the money from Mama's jewelry. As long as I'm careful with my finances I'll do all right. I've never asked anybody for anything and I don't intend to start now.

I stop sweeping. *But I guess I need to get a life.*

I haven't done much of anything since moving to Townsend. I'm all settled and ahead on purse-making, I don't have anything pressing to tend to, and the cramping eased up two weeks ago, so I'm feeling okay. I hadn't needed to see a doctor after all, thank goodness. The last thing I had wanted was to answer questions I knew I would have been asked.

With all of that behind me, I have no excuse for not getting out now and becoming a little more acquainted with the place.

A Different Forest

I have never read the *Christy* series, but I have seen the television show and the follow-up movies. As much as I liked it, I never thought I would visit the actual place the story was based on. But here I am.

It seems the passage of time has changed little of the land. The surrounding forests look untouched, wild roses dotting the countryside, making the scene look like one of those paintings I used to see in the window of an art gallery in Asheville. Looking around the site, so rich with history, I imagine Leonora Whitaker's (aka Christy) arrival taking the people by surprise. Mostly

German, Scottish and Irish immigrants, the people chose to live in the secluded Tennessee mountains rather than deal with outsiders. Right now, I can definitely relate.

There are signs marking the sites where the buildings once were: David Grantland's Bunkhouse (his real name was Reverend John Wood, the man Leonora eventually married,) the Mission Home, Minnie Fish's Cabin (Ruby Mae in the book.) Beyond these spots, the land is beautifully untamed.

My last stop is the Fish Cemetery where Minnie is buried.

Dragging my gaze from the gravestones and scanning the deep woods surrounding me, I imagine the mountain children running amok, playing hide-n-seek in the ancient forest and dodging trees, their faces dirty, their eyes wild with the innocent excitement of youth.

I close my eyes and sigh. How I envy that freedom–the kind of freedom that is no longer mine to enjoy.

Because I ran through the forest once . . .

Old Fort

"Where we going, Danny?"

"We goin' home, just takin' a scenic route. I wanna show you somethin'."

"Okay, but we better hurry. Dina's waitin', and you know how she gets when you're late for supper. With both of us late, she'll blow a gasket for sure."

"I told her I had a stop to make after pickin' you up, so stop worryin'."

"Thanks for the ride. I wasn't too keen on walkin' from Mary's"

"When is that woman gonna get that old hunka junk car fixed?"

"Soon as she gets the money."

"As little as she charges at that beauty salon, that'll be never."

"She's doin' all right."

My brother-in-law smirks, then turns down a dirt road into a heavily wooded area.

"Where we goin'?"

"I told ya, I wanna show you somethin." He pulls off the side of the road and parks. The sky is darkening, but there's still enough light for me to make out his hooded-eyed

expression. "So how about you pay up for the ride?"

"What?"

"You heard me," he says, laying a big hand on my thigh. I shove it away. "Come on, girl, you know this here has been a long time comin'."

"What?" I stare at him in horror. His smile is threatening to split his pudgy face in two. At six-foot-two and three hundred pounds, he's built like a linebacker. In fact, he played football in high school and a little in college before he dropped out. That's how he won Dina over. She was always a sucker for an athlete. That was five years ago.

"Danny, take me home."

"I will after I sample your wares."

Backing way, I reach for the door handle, but he grabs my arm.

"Where you think you goin', girl?"

"Let me go!" His grip is solid and I can't break free. "Let me go! Let me go!" Leaning down, I manage to bite his hand hard enough to draw blood and he yelps, his grip loosening enough for me to open the door and take off running.

"Get back here, girl!

The anger in his voice quickens my pace. Adrenaline

pumping through my insides, I weave through the trees, kicking up dry leaves with each step. I can't let him catch me because I know what will happen if he does.

I should have seen this coming. This past year I've noticed his occasional glances, his dark eyes roaming over my body, making me feel dirty at times. Lately, he has grown bolder, winking at me from across the kitchen table during supper, licking his lips suggestively. Standing in my way in our small kitchen so I have no choice but to brush against him to get by. Yeah, I should've seen this coming. So many times I have wanted to say something to Dina, but I knew she would be mad at me, not him. He knew it, too, so there has been nothing to stop him.

"Girl, when I catch you, you really got it comin'!"

I keep running.

"Dina's gonna be mad at you for makin' us late! Stop playin' and get on back here!"

Tired and growing more scared by the second, my lungs are burning, but I keep going. You would think as big as he is, he would be tired, too, but his voice doesn't sound tired. If anything, he sounds like he's just taking a leisurely stroll. Must be the residual effects of football training, even after all these years.

Finally ducking behind a large tree, I stop to catch my breath.

But this is a mistake. A moment later a meaty hand yanks my hair, snapping my head back.

"I told you to stop, didn't I? And you did, so that must mean you wantin' somethin'."

As I struggle to get away, he hits me and slams me to the ground. Fighting him off is useless, but I keep trying. Pinning me with his heavy body, he yanks down my pants, and, showing no mercy, brutally steals my innocence. All I can do is cry. It seems like a lifetime that I lay trapped under him, listening to his heavy breathing, his weight practically suffocating me. I stare up at the dark sky, tears blurring my vision of the stars peeking through the trees. Finally, it is over.

Limping back with tears streaming down my cheeks, dried leaves caught in my hair and dirt on my clothes, his final words echo in the swelling silence of the car as we head home.

"You better not tell anyone. If you do, you'll be sorry. And Dina won't believe you anyway."

* * *

"Are you all right?"

Eyes popping open, I jump, biting back a scream. I hadn't even heard the stranger approach. Wiping the tears from my face, I nod. "I'm fine."

"I didn't mean to intrude. I come up here every now and then." He chuckles. "I admit I'm a *Christy* fan. This is always my final stop. I think it's the most peaceful spot up here."

"It is peaceful," I agree, not looking at him, the tension inside me increasing by the second. I move away from Minnie Fis's grave, the sudden urge to run growing stronger.

"Don't leave. Please." His voice is soft.

Pausing, I finally glance at his face. He looks Native Indian, but not. His accent is definitely not American. Striking hazel eyes stare from an incredibly handsome face, light stubble covering his chiseled jaw. His wavy dark locks are tousled by the breeze. He doesn't seem threatening, but looks can be deceiving.

"I need to get back anyway."

"I'm really sorry to intrude upon your time."

"You didn't. But I ain't one to be standin' in the woods talkin' to a complete stranger, so I'd best be goin'." I quickly turn to leave, wanting to put as much distance between us as possible.

"Well," he calls after me, "if we should meet again, my name is Kellen. Kellen Youngblood."

Youngblood? The name is familiar, but I don't answer, I just keep walking until I reach my car. Locking the doors, I start the engine and head home.

Name Please?

Having spent the morning making purses, I sew the final stitches into the last shoulder bag. The patterns of red and white log cabin designs interspersed with blocks of blue and red flowers give the bag a look that is both patriotic and festive.

Crafted bags lay in a pile at my feet. I have been so engrossed in my work, I lost count of how many I've finished. Releasing a deep breath, I examine a few, checking the stitches, making sure they are straight. Though I love all the colorful fabrics, my favorite of the finished pieces is a large tote fashioned with quilted blocks of a bear family. The mama, papa and baby are smiling with arms laced together. The fabric makes me smile, bringing to mind happier times, times I shared with Mama. Mama and Mrs. Tilly were my two favorite people in the world. How I miss them both.

Old Fort

"Add a little more flour. That's right, now spread it out and leave it thick."

"How's this, Mama?" I mash the cutter into the dough she just talked me through.

"That's just fine, baby. Now put em' on the pan, but spray it with oil first."

When I finally put the pan in the oven, Mrs. Tilly says, "You gonna master your mama's biscuits yet. You about to eighteen, ain't you?" She is sitting at the table, nursing a glass of sweet tea.

"Just a month away, Mrs. Tilly."

"You gonna make a fine wife for the man lucky enough to get you." I roll my eyes because she says this frequently. "Time sure flies, don't it?"

"That is does," Mama says, sitting down next to Mrs. Tilly.

While the women talk, I clean up the flour and wipe off the counter, warmed by their comfortable chatter. It's a familiar sound I have listened to for as long as Mrs. Tilly has lived in the neighborhood. The scent of baking biscuits fills the kitchen and I inhale deeply, my mind conjuring up a picture of myself in a kitchen of my own, rolling out biscuits. A pair of muscular arms enfold me. The owner's face is unclear, but the scent of his cologne as he nuzzles his face against my neck is distinct, and one that belongs only to him, a scent I would definitely recognized if I ever smelled it.

"Where are you, girl?" comes Mama's voice.

"I'm here."

Mama says nothing, she simply smiles like she knows my secret thoughts. I think she does because she has always been able to read me like a book. This is a touching moment between us, one that I will never again get to share with her.

Later, she complains of yet another stomach ache and doubles over. We take her to the emergency room where they discover a cancerous tumor on one of her ovaries. The next week she has surgery but never improves. She grows sicker, her decline steady. With Dina and Danny both working long hours, I am left to care for her during the day.

Then she dies and my world changes forever. Two days later, her funeral is attended by half of Old Fort. So many people loved her and were shocked and saddened by her death. But no one could possibly be more shocked than me. At the graveside service, I sit between Mrs. Tilly and Mr. Tilly, listening to him murmur the same thing over and over.

"She shouldn't have died. She shouldn't have died . . ."

Mrs. Tilly repeatedly pats my hand saying, "It'll all come out in the wash," and I sit wondering what they mean, but too emotionally drained to ask.

Three months later, my sister leaves. Then the day eventually comes when my world is violently ripped apart, and I'm soon forced to leave as well.

* * *

Did you know, Kelly? Was Danny that way with you first? Is that why you left? Did he do to you what he did to me?

There are no answers to the internal questions I have harbored for months now. And until I finally hear from my sister, there won't be. I have considered trying to find her, but not knowing where to begin, I console myself with the belief that she is okay and will contact me eventually. She has always been a fighter and fiercely independent. She will call or write when she's ready.

I have got to get out of here. Putting my sewing supplies away, I grab my car keys.

* * *

"Hello again."

"Hey."

I have been standing next to Minnie Fish's grave again for the last five minutes, contemplating the life of the people who once lived in these mountains. I managed to put the earlier pondering of my own life out of my mind, if only for a while. I never expected to see him again. It has been a month since I was here last. The leaves have begun changing to their various colors and the scent of fall is in the air, which at the moment includes a whiff of skunk perfume. I sure hope the critter gives us a wide berth as it passes.

"I am intruding again. Would you like to be alone?"

"No," I admit honestly, surprising myself. I've had plenty of time alone and I'm tired. He seems safe, I'm not sure. I'm not sure about much of anything anymore. "I'm okay."

"Well, we aren't strangers anymore. At least I'm not to you. But you on the other hand . . ."

A smile burst forth before I can stop it. "Is this your sneaky way of learnin' my name?"

"I would never be so underhanded as to try to trick you. I'm simply pointing out that you know me, but I don't know you. Wait . . . I shouldn't be talking to strangers out here in the woods."

"If you wanna know my name, all you gotta do is ask." He smiles but doesn't say anything. "Well?"

"Well what?"

"Ain't you gonna ask me?"

"Hmmm, I'm thinking maybe I don't want to know."

"Humph, okay then. It was nice talkin' to you." I turn to leave.

"Wait, don't go."

"Why not?"

"It's rude to leave your new acquaintance standing out here alone. I mean, what if I'm mauled by a bear or skunk or something?"

I allow my gaze to travel over his lean muscular physique. "I'm sure you could take em'." Smiling slightly, I start walking away again.

"But what if you get attacked then? I'll need to

protect you."

"I didn't think of that." I give him a teasing grin. "Think you can handle em'?

"I think so. But first I need to know the name of the person in my care." He holds out a hand.

Hesitating only a moment, I timidly place my hand in his, shaking it as he gently closes his fingers around mine. "Sonora. Sonora Kingston."

"It's a pleasure to finally meet you, Sonora."

"You too."

"You sure don't make it easy."

"And I don't intend to."

"I figured that. Luckily I'm a patient man."

"Is that right?"

"Yes. And if you give me a chance, you beautiful little forest sprite, I'll show you just how patient."

He has the most adorable smile I've ever seen. "Forest sprite?"

"Yes." He arches a brow. "With that gorgeous honey-blond hair and those striking violet eyes, and standing at what, four-feet-nine or ten? You look like a forest sprite to me–that is, if they actually exist." He grins, winking at me. "You're an adorable little thing and you've enchanted the whole area."

I laugh. "You are somethin', you know that?"

"Oh, you have no idea."

Family Connections

Three weeks later.

How do you fight what feels like fate? How do you keep your heart closed and your off-limits emotions from abandoning what they vowed to never allow?

The simple answer is you don't. You let go of the rope in the emotional tug-of-war and save yourself some agonizing blisters that are inevitable. Fighting what seems meant to be is too exhausting.

Sitting on the screened porch, I pull the heavy sweater tighter around me and ponder the changes that have come into my life–changes that testify of my mental ramblings. I am waiting for Kellen to pick me up. We are driving to Old Fort. I've heard it said many times that this is a small world, and each time, I have just nodded and smiled. But since discovering mine and Kellen's mutual connection in the town of my birth, I've now come to believe that saying.

Three weeks ago.

Having finished our meal, we top it off with pecan pie and cold lemonade. The diner is all but empty, so we have the whole section to ourselves. Since leaving the Fish cemetery, conversation has been slow. I know I need to open up a bit, but I don't know how. Self-preservation has become ingrained and I have to wonder if there will ever come a time when that isn't the case. With Kellen's introduction a month ago came the introduction of change, something I hadn't the faintest idea was happening, nor had I been prepared for it.

"So how long have you lived in Townsend?" Kellen asks after swallowing a bite of pie.

"A couple of months."

"Do you like it?"

"I like it fine."

"Where did you move from?"

"Old Fort."

"Really? My mother and step-father moved to Old Fort from Knoxville about ten years ago. My mother was born and raised there."

"No kiddin'?"

"They really like it there."

"Forgive me for askin', but where are you from? And what race are you? Your accent definitely ain't American"

He smiles. "You're forgiven. My mother is Cherokee. My father is from India, but his father was Navajo and his mother Indian. That's where the Youngblood name comes from. So I guess you could say I'm double Indian."

I chuckle. "I'm kind of partial to the Cherokee people."

"You are? Why is that?"

"Well, an old friend that I love almost as much as my mama is Cherokee. She passed on about a month before I moved here."

"Hmmm, I'm curious. What was her name?"

"Why?" My defenses instantly rise.

"I only ask because my mother passed away around that time."

Taking a second to kick myself, I answer, "Her name

was Mrs. Josephine Tilly." When his eyes widen, I gasp. "No way! Mrs. Tilly was your mama?"

"She was. Carlton is my stepfather."

"I can't believe it! Mrs. Tilly was my favorite person in the world next to Mama. And Mr. Tilly, though he ain't ever said much to me really, he's a kind man. He always smiled whenever he saw me. Sometimes it seemed like a sad smile, but he smiled just the same."

"Yeah, that's Dad. Like my real father who passed away, Dad is a good man." He pauses. "Mom did tell me about losing her good friend. I'm sorry."

"Thanks."

"She said you have two sisters."

"Yeah. The youngest left a few months after Mama died and I haven't seen her since. My older sister . . . we don't get along too well."

"I'm sorry," he says again, and as I take in his kind expression, I can tell they aren't just words.

"You'll probably think I'm crazy, but I have felt your mama near me frequently since she passed on and . . . sometimes she has spoken to me." I arch a defiant brow, bracing myself for what he will say. However, his response is both surprising and unexpected.

"Then you can count yourself very blessed. For God to gift you with something so wonderful, you must be an amazing person indeed."

I smile shyly, warmed by his words. I am starting to feel a kinship with this man now. If only I had known him before. Of course, he's so much older than me, I doubt he would've paid me any attention. By my account, he would be around thirty-four or so, fourteen years older than me.

"I can't believe we have never met," I say. "All the pictures I've seen of you are when you were younger. Well, wait, there is a more recent picture of you on the Tilly's fireplace mantle, but it's kind of blurry and you were wearin' somethin' on your head. And your clothes were different."

"That photo was taken in India. I lived there with some of my father's family up until a few years ago."

"Now I know why your name sounded familiar when we met."

"It did, huh? Why didn't you say anything?"

"I don't know. I suppose because you were a stranger, remember?"

He grins. "How could I forget?"

His amused gaze makes me blush a little. "Well, what brought you here to Townsend?"

"I don't know really. When I decided to move back, I knew I didn't want to live in Old Fort with my parents. I had been on my own for too long and I needed space. I wanted to open a little shop and sell Indian and Native American gifts. There was an available space here, so I bought it and opened Indian Indian Gifts.*"*

"Indian Indian, *huh? That's catchy."*

"I thought so. We sell everything from sarees and Indian jewelry to moccasins, belts, and beaded Native American headwear, as well as other accessories."

"Sounds like a nice little shop."

"Tourists seem to like it. So what do you do?"

"I make quilted purses."

"Really? Where do you sell them?"

"At Cabin Crafts.*"*

"If you'd like, I would be glad to carry some at the shop. The more outlets you have, the better, don't you think?"

"I do. That would be nice. Thank you."

"You're welcome. Would you mind if I came by later to see your designs?"

I am hesitant to answer, not sure if I want him to know where I live just yet. At the same time, I know trust has got to start somewhere. I really like him. I didn't want to, but I do.

Sensing my hesitance, Kellen surprises me by saying softly, "Sonora, you are safe with me. I would never hurt you."

Does he know? He can't know. Do I look damaged? Yes, I'm a little damaged, but do I look it?

Looking into his earnest eyes, something inside me begins to relax, and somehow I know I can trust him. "All right," I finally answer.

Two weeks and ten dates later–the bulk of this time consisting of long evenings spent at Kellen's place and mine–we stand next to Minnie Fish's grave, where he draws me into his arms and we share our first kiss. His touch is gentle, as if he is handling something fragile and precious. Mere words could never describe what it feels like to be wrapped in Kellen's embrace while his sensuous mouth–a mouth I've stared at for hours–passionately explores mine. He feels divine, his kiss the taste of honeysuckle, his skin the scent of cinnamon and summer. The emotional moan that escapes him at the sensation of our tongues sweeping against one another and my hands in his tousled dark waves, and then his heart-felt words of, "I love you, Sonora. You're the reason I am here," completely shift my world, making it easy for me to respond, "I love you too." He smiles and simply holds me close, and I think to myself, This is what you meant, Mama, ain't it? This is how it's supposed to be between two people in love. *It is also during this moment that I realize the cologne he always wears matches the scent of the faceless man in my old daydreams. I know it's most likely my mind playing tricks on me, but that's okay. This is way better than the best dream.*

"You are the only man I'll ever feel safe in the woods with, you know?" He draws back a little at my words.

Stupid, stupid, Sonora! *I search for something to smooth over what I let slip. I'm not ready to tell him yet. One day I'll have to, but not today. "It's just that the woods aren't safe to be in alone, that's all."*

He studies me quietly and I have to look away. Then taking my face in his hands, he says, "I promise you, Sonora, I'll never let anything happen to you."

I rest my hand against his chest, feeling sinewy muscle beneath his shirt. "I believe you."

I glance at my watch. Kellen will be here any

minute now and we will be on our way. I only wish we were returning to Old Fort under happier circumstances.

Old Mr. Tilley had a stroke this morning and passed away on the way to the hospital. They called Kellen and he asked me to go back with him. Truthfully, I never wanted to set foot in that town again, and I hadn't planned to, but I could never leave Kellen to handle this alone. The moment he said, "You're all I have in this world, Sonora," I knew I would follow him anywhere.

When Kellen arrives, I take him in my arms, offering what comfort I can, my heart breaking as he holds on to me, crying against my shoulder. Then we kiss, and somehow I know–with everything that I am, I know–I will belong to this man forever.

Secrets

Three days later.

Following the funeral and potluck lunch, we head back to the Tilly's place, stopping for a moment in front of my old home. The place has been vacant for the past couple of months. One of the neighbors said Dina and Danny packed up some things and left the day after I did. I can't help wondering why she wanted me gone when they were planning on leaving anyway. I guess it goes back to what Mama always said about kids with toys. They might not want it, but they don't want you to have it either. It makes me sad to think I could have still been there and mama's flower garden wouldn't be dying. Then again, if I hadn't gone, I would never have met Kellen. Having him is worth losing the house.

After a few visitors have come and gone, we spend the rest of the afternoon boxing up the Tilly's personal belongings to take to the thrift store. Some things we throw away, like Mrs. Tilly's old gardening clothes and Mr. Tilly's muddy boots and work gloves. Anything that is broken or worn out is thrown away. Kellen keeps a few sentimental things and gives me Mrs. Tilly's jewelry. Each piece is precious to me and I will always treasure them.

I've always loved being in this house. The style is the same as my old home, as well as most of the other homes in the neighborhood. Two-story brick exterior with white siding and a long front porch. Mrs. Tilly's taste in decorating was almost the same as Mama's. But after Mama died, our home was never the same and the feeling there changed. I suppose that's why I came to love this house. There was so much love here, and there still is, even with the Tillys' absence.

Going through one of the bedside tables in their

room, I am surprised to find a letter-size envelope with my name on it. "Look at this," I say, showing it to Kellen.

He takes it and examines the handwriting. "Dad wrote this." His eyes meet mine. "It must be something important," he says handing it back to me.

What would he have to say to me? Sitting on the bed, I open the envelope and pull out the handwritten pages. Kellen sits next to me and wraps an arm around my waist. At the top of the first page is written, *My Confession.* Talk about an intimidating start!

Dear Sonora,

You have always been the sweetest young lady I have ever known. From the day we moved into this house and you rode by on your bike and smiled that innocent young smile, you ingrained yourself in my heart, carved your own little place there. You had no idea your smile was just what I needed that day. As Josephine and your mama got to know each other and became good friends, I grew to see the pureness of your spirit. I also grew very protective of you, almost like a father.

How well I remember the taunting you suffered from the neighborhood kids just before you became a teenager. I remember how the young boys began to buzz around you when you turned sixteen like flies to honey. Ah, you were a beauty! When you walked by, the boys stood a little taller and the sun shined brighter simply because you walked beneath it. I'll confess, me and Jo sort of hoped that when you grew up, you would meet our son and he'd fall madly in love with you . . .

Snatching my eyes from the letter, I look at Kellen, meeting his adorable grin.

"I guess they got their wish," he says, kissing my cheek.

"I guess so," I agree, awe filling me. I never knew Mr. Tilly liked me that much. I continue reading.

True, he's much older, but that doesn't matter. He's a good man, and age is nothing when the feelings are there. Always remember that, Sonora.

As I said, you were a beauty, and so was your sister, Kelly, and everybody noticed you. Then the wrong person started noticing you both.

Dina's husband would sit on the porch and

watch you when you stood outside, talking to your friends. I watched his eyes roaming over your body, following you whenever you walked by. He was dirty. He was scum, raping you with his very look.

Then your mama died and he grew bolder. One day I came up on him when he had your sister cornered by the side of the house. When I stopped and stared him down, he smiled and patted Kelly on the shoulder and said she could go. Then he tried to feed me some story about planning a surprise party for Dina and not wanting her to overhear. He must have taken me for a fool or something, because the look on your sister's face told me different. I felt sad because you girls no longer had anyone to watch out for you. This made me start trying to keep an eye on you even more. You couldn't even trust your own people. You should have been able to trust those closet to you, but you couldn't . .

I have to stop reading as a bout of emotion overtakes me. I can no longer see through the tears filling my eyes. They roll down my face, falling to the paper and Kellen takes the letter from me, pulling me to him. Burying my face against his chest, I cry, thinking about Kelly and what Danny put her through, understanding completely and feeling for her. No wonder she left.

Kellen presses a kiss to my brow, then draws back a little and I see the tears in his eyes. "Would you like me to read some?" he asks and I nod. Keeping one arm around me, he reads more of his father's words. His voice is soothing, its timbre rich and deep.

You know, I always found it peculiar how Millie died. After that surgery, she should have been fine. She shouldn't have died . . .

"He said that durin' Mama's graveside service," I say. "He murmured it over and over. Then your mama said, "It'll all come out in the wash." I wondered what they meant, but I was in so much pain over losin' Mama, I didn't ask."

Kellen is quiet for a moment. "Well, since the letter is entitled, *My Confession*, I think we're about to find out the answer to that question. And I have a feeling that's not all."

Shuddering, I take a moment to soak in his warmth, contemplating what we've read so far before nodding for him to continue.

Anyway, me and Jo started mulling things over, but we couldn't come up with anything, we just knew something wasn't right. Then one day, Kellie came out of the house with a backpack. She got in the car with Dina and they drove away. She saw me sitting on the front porch and waved through the back window. She was finally getting away and I was glad, but I knew how hurt you would be to come home and find her gone.

Then things started getting worse for you. We knew it without you saying a thing. And I knew it was only a matter of time before he tried something. Then he did. The night you came to Jo and told her what happened, she couldn't sleep until she told me. I immediately punched a hole in the wall, then I sat down and cried. She said she begged you to go to the police, but you were too scared. And you knew Dina would side with him.

A month after my sweet Jo passed on, I saw the truth of what you told her. I watched your sister kick you out and tell you not to come back. She sided with her good-for-nothing husband against you. You were in pain that day. I knew you were, and I knew why. I

*wanted to go to you and say you could stay here, but–
and you will probably think I'm crazy–but Jo came to
me and said to let you go. She said she would help you
get where you need to go . . .*

Kellen stops, raising his eyes to mine. "Your
sister's husband . . . you mean he . . . did he . . . "

"He did," I admit, grateful to finally share the
truth without having to say the words. The letter had
done that.

"Oh, Sonora!" he whispers, again pulling me to
him, holding me tightly. "Oh, baby," he rasps against
my ear. "No wonder you didn't trust me when you met
me." I silently cling to him, burying my face against his
neck. Drawing back after a moment, he wipes his face
and finally smiles. "At least you know for sure now
that you aren't crazy. Mama really was there for you."

I smile, grateful for the confirmation through Mr.
Tilly's letter. "And she led me to you."

"A fact that just blows my mind," he says. "She
and Dad were determined."

"And I'm glad they succeeded."

"So am I." He is about to start reading again but
stops. "What did he mean by you being in pain?"

I drop my eyes, but he lifts my chin, urging me to look at him. "Tell me, honey. You can tell me anything."

Taking a deep breath, I say, "I was pregnant. I lost the baby that day." Now that the door has opened, I share the entire experience with him, from the day of the rape to the day I left.

Saying nothing, Kellen simply gathers me to him, but not before I see the tears that quickly streak his face. He holds me in silence, burying his face in my hair, and I can feel him collecting his emotions, getting them under control.

"If that man was still around here, I think I would kill him. And your sister wouldn't get away with her part in this either."

"Well, as your mama said, it'll all come out in the wash one day. God sees everything and He will take care of them both one day."

"I'm sure you're right." Kissing my brow once more, he holds me close another moment before continuing.

Sonora, it literally killed me to see you walking down that road alone, not knowing where you would go or how you would get there. I knew where you were going, but you didn't. Jo told me, then she said you needed her and she left.

Late that night, I crept around to the back of your house (I still considered it yours because I knew Millie meant for you to be there.) The kitchen window was open and I heard them talking and laughing. And what I heard was so heinous, I can't even give words to it. I can't even write it down.

I went back home, locked the door, then dropped to my knees by the bed and cried.

The dead could no longer talk.

I could.

But I didn't.

I'm so sorry.

Please forgive me . . .

"What the hell . . ." Kellen springs from the bed. "That's it?" he cries, reading his father's final words again. "That's it? He died without telling anyone what he knew? What did he hear?"

"I don't know," I say, just as stumped as he is. I take the letter from him and read over the last part again. "I don't understand. Why didn't he tell me? Why didn't he finish? How could he leave me wonderin' what happened?"

Kellen shoves a hand back through his hair, his face angry. Then he looks at me and his expression sobers. Taking my hand, we walk into the living room and stare through the window at my abandoned old home. "I'm so sorry," he says, drawing me in his arms.

"I know," I sigh. "Me too. I just wish I knew what he knew. If only to have some closure." Closing my eyes, I lay my head against his chest, calmed by his strong heartbeat. We hold each other in silence, our words used up.

The Truth

A hard thump against the door startles us both. Releasing me, Kellen opens it to find no one there.

"Must have been some kid."

"They couldn't have disappeared that fast." A puzzled look creases his brow. "Where did those come from?" I ask, looking down on the porch.

"Hey, I thought I threw these away," he says, picking up Mr. Tilly's muddy boots.

Staring at the boots, my heart slowly begins to thump. I look up at him as a familiar warmth rushes over me. "You did." I watch the color drain from his face. Casting my eyes upward, I whisper, "What are you tryin' to tell us, Mrs. Tilly?"

There is no response, but a picture appears in my head that causes me to tremble and I back into the doorway. "No, Mrs. Tilly."

"What is it?" Kellen asks, taking my hand.

I can't answer him. I just frantically shake my head. "No, Mrs. Tilly. I can't."

You have to, baby.

Hot tears spill down my cheeks. "I can't go back there."

"Go back where?" Kellen presses, his voice rising a pitch.

The answers are there.

"But I can't."

You won't be alone, baby. My boy will be right there with you.

I grip Kellen's hand in both of mine, squeezing so tightly he almost winces. "Grab your keys. We need to go."

"Where?"

"Please," I whisper, fear slicing through me, "get your keys."

* * *

The sun is slowly sinking as we walk quickly through the woods. Kellen's arm is securely wrapped around my trembling shoulders, but that doesn't stop the flashes of that terrible night from seizing me. Kellen had been mortified when I told him where we were going, and had tried to talk me out of coming, but deep down he knew his mama was leading us to the truth and there was no other choice.

As we rush through the trees, I can almost feel them remembering what happened there. The giant oaks witnessed things no one else had, and one day, just like the mountains, they will testify of those things.

When we finally arrive at the place, the sight before me literally makes my heart stop. Kellen inhales sharply, neither of us uttering a word.

Before us lay two mounds of dirt, both about as long as a grave. Beyond them lies a third, only it looks older. Each mound is marked with a white stone about eight inches wide. As we approach, the words painted on them in small print become clear.

One reads: **Here lies a murderer and rapist.**

The second reads: **Here lies his accomplice.**

As I approach the third older grave, a river of tears run down my face.

Here lies Kelly Kingston, their victim, and one of the sweetest souls to ever grace this earth.

Immediately after reading it, I turn in Kellen's arms and cry, aware of him crying with me. A new wave of griefs hits me, only this time it is for Kelly. Even though we've been apart, I have always taken comfort in knowing she was somewhere out there in the world. Now that comfort is gone and an emptiness is left.

As I stand wrapped in Kellen's embrace, like a movie screen is suddenly thrust before me, I see everything that happened. When Kellen gasps, I know he is seeing it, too.

Mr. Tilly putting on gloves and slipping through the unlocked back door in the middle of the night.

Turning on a small flashlight, pulling out his gun and shooting Dina point blank.

Interrogating a sobbing Danny and being told exactly where he raped, killed and buried Kelly.

Danny admitting he and Dina poisoned Mama to get the house and what money she left.

Danny admitting he raped me near where he murdered Kelly. He says Dina knew everything and wanted me out of the house.

Mr. Tilly shooting Danny in the head, wrapping them both in sheets, covering them in garbage sacks, then dragging their bodies to his waiting car.

Mr. Tilly driving out to where Kelly is buried and digging two more graves.

Pulling out a small can of paint. Taking the stones from a canvas bag.

And finally, Mr. Tilly falling to the living room floor just days ago, clutching his heart.

A New Beginning

A month later.

This morning we were married on the screened porch with no one present but the reverend. And we were sure, somewhere near, was Mrs. Tilly.

Now, in the bedroom among my packed belongings, Kellen makes love to me, restoring what was brutally taken from me, and gifting me with the kind of love that should have been mine in the first place. Each sensation–the touch of his hands, the taste of his kiss, the scent of his skin, the feel of his mouth against my own skin, and the warmth of his body wrapping around mine–is new, yet somehow familiar, like my very being has always known his, and always belonged to him. His touch heals the hurt from the past and takes the pain away. When we become one, for a moment the world stops moving, the earth grows still, then suddenly galaxies are created from the explosive power of what is between us. Nothing in this earthly sphere can, or will, ever compare to the bliss we find in each other's arms.

The following day we move my things to my new home. The home Kellan has owned for the past few years sits high in the mountains with plenty of windows to take in the view from every direction. It is rugged but beautiful, and I look forward to the memories I will make here with him.

* * *

We spend many evenings on the back deck, watching deer beyond the fence, and squirrels and chipmunks scale the trees surrounding us. Many of these moments find us contemplating our life and pondering the events that brought us together. I would never wish my past on anyone, but neither would I wish it away. Every step I have ever taken, everything that has ever happened in my life, every joy, every pain, every trial and triumph, have only served to lead me here. Here to share a life with this man. A life of beauty, wonder, passion, and love.

As the skies darken and the stars appear, Kellen's arms warm me against the chill.

"I love you," he says, taking my mouth with his, gifting me with a kiss filled with the sensuality that is so him.

"I love you too."

"And I'm glad Mom sent you to Townsend," he murmurs against my lips.

I smile. "You and me both."

"How about letting me show you how glad?"

"Ain't you doin' that now?"

"Oh, I'm just getting warmed up, my little forest sprite." He grins, lifting me and carrying me into the house.

* * *

Kellen

Kellen Youngblood has traveled the world and seen great beauty, but never has he seen anything more beautiful than Sonora lying beneath the bedroom skylight, bathed in the moonlight above them, gazing up at him with eyes full of love, her soul completely bare to him. She is so tiny, he sometimes feels like he is handling a porcelain doll. However, he knows she isn't as breakable as she looks. She is the strongest person he has ever known, and he is the most blessed man in the world to own her heart, to have her own his in return.

From the moment Kellen came upon Sonora in the Fish Cemetery, he wanted her for his own. He has always considered himself a sensible guy, never prone to acting irrationally, but the moment he met Sonora, all rational thought left him, and it was all he could do not to declare his heart that day. She had been skittish, and the last thing he'd wanted was to frighten her away. When she left–almost running–she took a chunk of his heart with her. He'd spent the following month thinking about her, his 'little forest sprite,' and prayed he would see her again. And then one day she was there, looking even more beautiful than the first time he saw her. She sealed her place in his soul that day, leaving a permanent brand that would never fade.

Discovering the connection between them was nothing short of amazing. He had decided to take things slow and get to know her, and he eventually came to know her better than anyone else in his life. By the time he kissed her for the first time, he was so hopelessly in love, he couldn't bear being away from her.

Then his father passed away and all the hidden secrets were laid open before them both. So much death, so many lies, all the pain and heartache. It had been hard for Kellen to see what had become of his stepfather. Though Kellen could understand Carlton's love for Sonora, her sister and her mother, and understand what drove him to such violent acts, he could never imagine actually doing something like that. His mother knew. She knew what would happen and had been with Sonora through it all. And his mother and stepfather got their wish. He and Sonora met and he fell in love with her. That Sonora managed to come through it all with her emotions intact was a miracle, one that he will be eternally grateful for.

And now she is his wife.

As Sonora's arms come around him, Kellen melts against her, worshiping her body, again thanking the heavens that he is no longer alone. He'd spent far too many years alone, wondering if there was anyone out there for him. He'd only needed to move from India to Tennessee and exercise patience.

"I love you," he whispers against her skin.

She breathes, "I love you too," and Kellen's eyes burn as happy tears fill them.

* * *

You will never find a more content person than me.

Mama used to say, "A heart may be broken, but it beats just the same." Kellen tells me I am living proof of that saying. He's absolutely right. Emotionally, I may have been down for a time, but I was never knocked out. I found a second wind in the mountains at the Fish Cemetery. Who knows? Maybe old Minnie had a hand in things, too.

I won't question it. I am just glad for it.

Clutching a Beating Heart

About the Author

J. (Jewel) Adams stays crazy busy with her family and writing. She has written several books in different genres and is also a motivational speaker to both youth and adult audiences.

In her spare time (when she has any) she likes to curl up with a good book and a healthy stash of orange Tic Tacs. She and her family reside in Utah.

Jewel loves hearing from her fans. You can contact her at jewela40@gmail.com

Visit Jewels Blog at jewelsbestgems.blogspot.com

Books by J. Adams/Jewel Adams

Mercedes' Mountain
The Journey
Place In This World
Tears of Heaven
Against the Odds
Still His Woman
The Wishing Hour
Guardian of My Heart
The Legacy
That Kind of Love
New
Say What You Need to Say
Beautiful In My Eyes
Sweet 21 Birthday Ball
For Love of Angel
The Passionate Hearts Novelette Collection
Letters In the Moonlight of Taj Mahal
Like the Wind

Forbidden Portals: The Quicksilver Project
Forbidden Portals: The Quicksilver Clones
Stories of the Heart
Out of the Closet Into the Light